Library-Media Center
Hanover Elementary School
274 Labeauxe Avenue
Hanover, MN 55341

PROTECTING RIVERS & SEAS

Kamini Khanduri

Edited by Felicity Brooks

Designed by Mary Cartwright

Illustrated by Steven Kirk, Peter Chesterton and Peter Bull

Series consultant: David Duthie

Contents

2	All about water	16	Hunting and collecting
4	Freshwater habitats	18	Changing habitats
6	Living in the ocean	20	Working towards a safer world
8	Sea shores and coral reefs	22	What you can do
10	Pollution	24	Index
12	More pollution		
14	Dangers from fishing		

Conservation consultant: Judy Oglethorpe

All about water

All living things need water to survive. On Earth, there is plenty. Water covers two-thirds of the planet's surface. The seas and oceans contain salt water. The rivers, lakes, streams and ponds contain fresh water. In this book, you can find out why the world's water is now in danger, and how we can protect it.

The planet Earth looks blue from space because there is so much water on it.

Pacific Ocean

The water cycle

There is no new water. The same water keeps moving between sea, air and land. This movement is called the water cycle. The picture below shows how it works.

1. Rain comes from clouds. When it falls on to land, a lot of it runs into streams and lakes.

2. Streams run together to form rivers.

3. Heat from the sun makes some of the water in lakes and rivers turn into a gas called water vapour.

4. Rivers flow into the sea.

5. Water from the surface of the sea also turns into water vapour.

6. When it begins to cool, water vapour turns into tiny water droplets. Millions of these join together to form clouds.

Water vapour rises.

Water vapour rises.

The areas near where rivers come out into the sea are called estuaries.

When salt water turns into water vapour, the salt is left behind.

Groundwater

Some rainwater collects underground too. It seeps through soil and into rock that has tiny holes in it. This water is called groundwater.

A plant's roots take up water from the soil. Most of it passes back into the air from its leaves.

Living in water

Many plants and animals live in or near water. The place where a plant or animal lives is called its habitat. Below are some water habitats. You can find out about the wildlife living there on pages 4-9.

Rivers

Oceans

Sea shores

Coral reefs

Pollution

Many water habitats are being polluted because people dump waste in them. Water pollution does not always stay in one place. It can be carried from streams to rivers, or from rivers to seas.

The River Rhine, for example, flows from the Alps to the North Sea. On its way, it runs through several countries. Factories along the river's banks dump their waste into the water. By the time it reaches the sea, the river is badly polluted.

Few plants and animals can live in polluted water.

Water facts

★ Only a tiny amount of the Earth's water is fresh water. Most of this is under the ground, or frozen into ice.

★ Each person needs to drink about 1,000 litres (2,100 pints) of water a year.

★ Water makes up nearly three-quarters of a person's body weight.

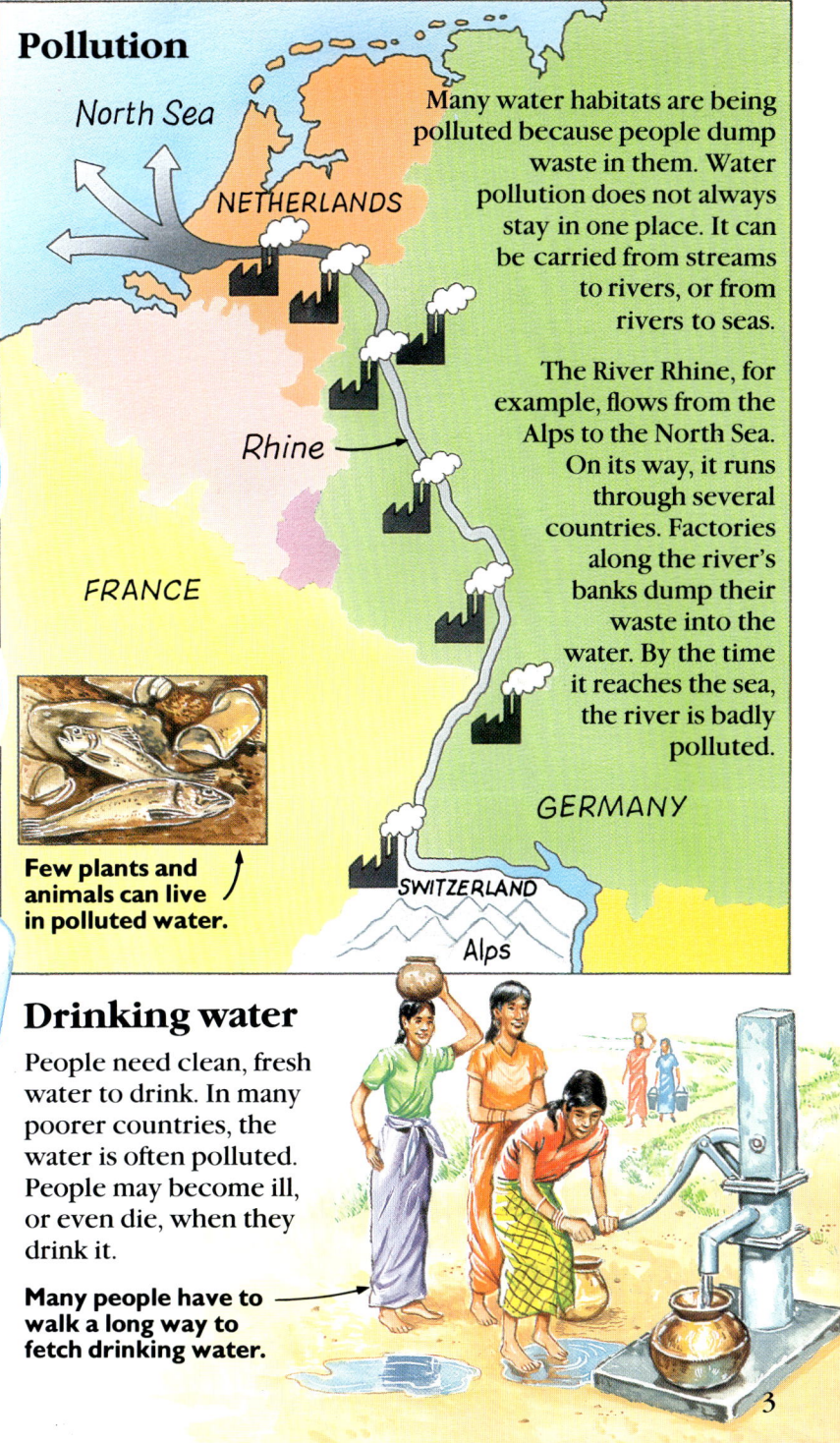

Drinking water

People need clean, fresh water to drink. In many poorer countries, the water is often polluted. People may become ill, or even die, when they drink it.

Many people have to walk a long way to fetch drinking water.

Freshwater habitats

All kinds of wildlife live in or beside fresh water. Many are now in danger from pollution, and because their habitats are being destroyed by humans.

River homes

These are some of the animals and plants that live in or beside a European river. They are all suited, or adapted, to this habitat.

Wetlands

Wetlands are areas of land which are often covered by water. Swamps, marshes and estuaries are all wetlands. Wetlands are home to a great number of different kinds of plants and animals. Here are some of them.

Hippopotamuses live in African swamps.

Marsh crocodiles live in India and Sri Lanka.

Dragonflies lay their eggs in water. After hatching, dragonfly nymphs stay in the water until they turn into adults.

Dragonfly nymph

Adult dragonfly

Reeds

Willow tree

Bulrushes

Kingfishers sit on branches above the water. They dive down to catch fish from the river below.

Otters live near water, in holes in the ground. They swim very well, and catch fish and other small animals, such as frogs.

Fish

Many kinds of fish live in fresh water. Different fish eat different things, so they are not all looking for the same food.

Carp eat insects.

Salmon spend most of their lives in the sea but they swim up rivers to lay their eggs.

Perch eat small fish.

Bitterling eat plants.

Wetland food chain

In every habitat, animals and plants are linked by a food chain, with animals depending on plants, or on other animals, for food. Below you can see the way that some animals and plants are linked in a wetland food chain.

Stork
Many birds use wetlands as resting places on their long journeys.

Cordgrass is eaten by freshwater shrimps. → Freshwater shrimps are eaten by eels. → Eels are eaten by storks.

Beavers

Beavers live in family groups, in Europe and North America. They build homes, called lodges, in streams and rivers. They also build dams, to widen the stream or river into a pond. This stops other animals from reaching the lodge, and harming the beavers.

Inside the lodge
- Beavers' living area
- Underwater food store
- Lodge entrance

Lodges and dams are made of sticks, stones and mud.

Lodge
Dam

Beavers cut down trees with their sharp front teeth. They use the wood for building and the bark for food.

Frogs and toads

Frogs and toads live both in water and on land. Most lay their eggs in fresh water.

Golden toads are only found in Costa Rica, but none have been seen since 1989.

Pine Barrens tree frogs live in North American swamps. Their homes are now being destroyed.

Surinam toads carry their eggs on their backs, until they grow into tiny toads.

Eggs

Living in the ocean

Seas and oceans are large areas of salt water. They make up nine-tenths of the water on Earth. Many animals living in seas and oceans are now in great danger from pollution of their habitats, and from hunting and fishing.

Cold-water animals

The Arctic and Southern Oceans contain very cold water. Here are some of the animals that are adapted to survive there.

Polar bears live in the Arctic Ocean, and on the ice there. They are very good swimmers. They feed on fish and seals.

White fur helps to keep polar bears hidden against the ice and snow.

Penguins cannot fly but they are excellent swimmers. This helps them to catch fish in the water.

Penguins use their narrow wings as flippers.

Seals cannot breathe underwater, but some can stay under for up to half an hour. Seals eat fish and shellfish.

A thick layer of fat under the skin keeps seals warm in icy water.

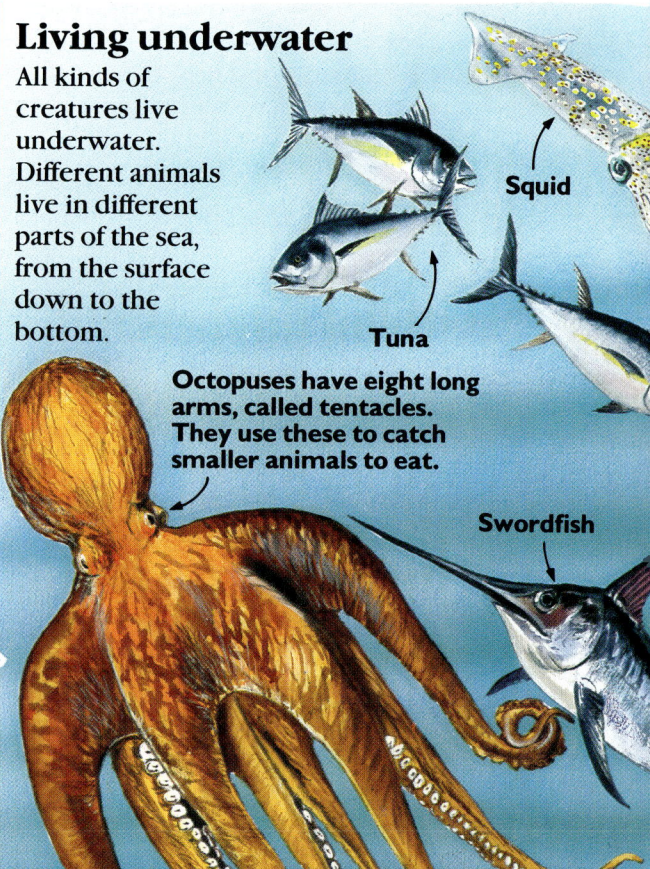

Living underwater

All kinds of creatures live underwater. Different animals live in different parts of the sea, from the surface down to the bottom.

Squid

Tuna

Octopuses have eight long arms, called tentacles. They use these to catch smaller animals to eat.

Swordfish

Plankton are tiny plants and animals that live near the surface. Larger animals, such as whales and fish, eat them. Plankton are very important in the ocean food chain.

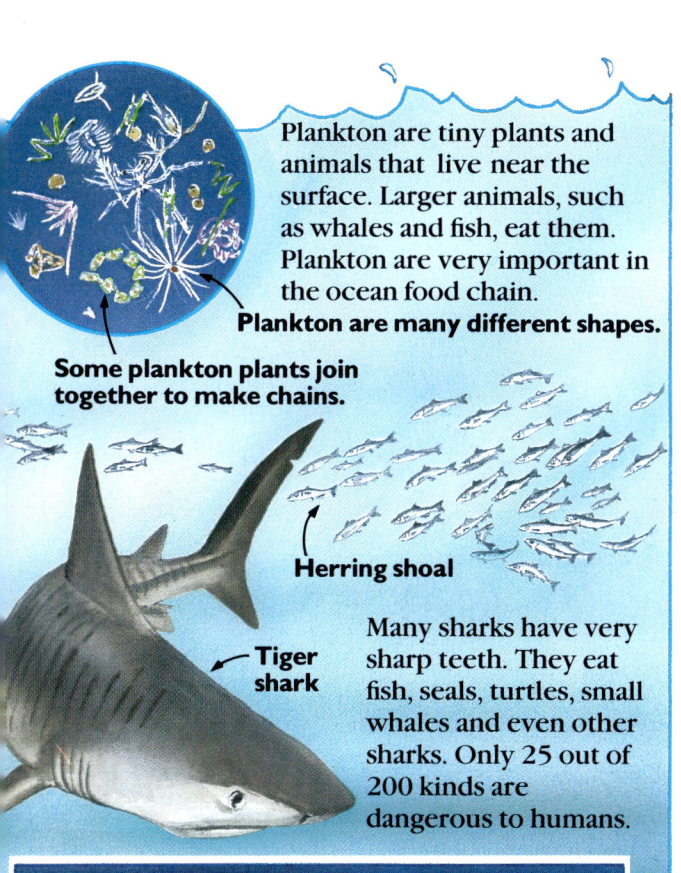

Plankton are many different shapes.

Some plankton plants join together to make chains.

Herring shoal

Tiger shark

Many sharks have very sharp teeth. They eat fish, seals, turtles, small whales and even other sharks. Only 25 out of 200 kinds are dangerous to humans.

Whales

Whales live in the sea, but have to swim to the surface to breathe. There are more than 80 different kinds. Whales are very intelligent animals. Many of them are in danger from hunting and pollution.

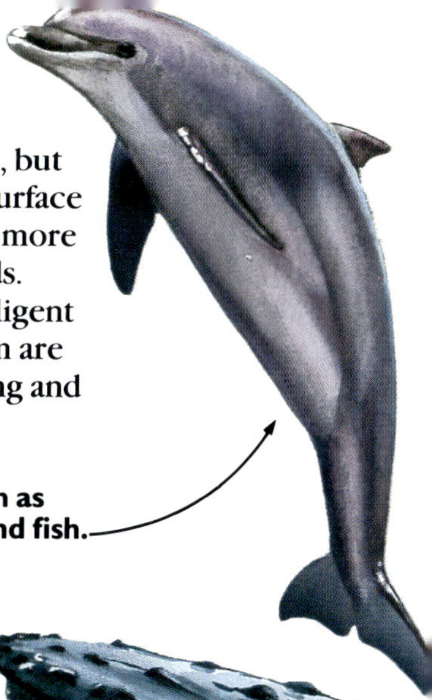

Toothed whales, such as dolphins, eat squid and fish.

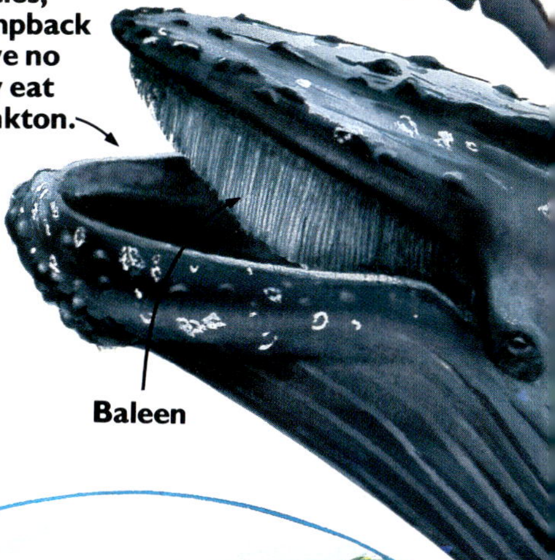

Baleen whales, such as humpback whales, have no teeth. They eat animal plankton.

They sieve the plankton into their mouths through fringes of tough skin, called baleen.

Baleen

Deep water

It is cold and dark in the deepest parts of the ocean. Some animals living there have unusual ways of finding food. A deep-sea angler fish can light up the lure on its head (see below). Smaller animals swim towards the light and the angler fish catches them in its mouth.

Lure

Exploring underwater

There are still many discoveries to be made about life in the ocean. Scientists use underwater ships, called submersibles, to explore the deepest parts.

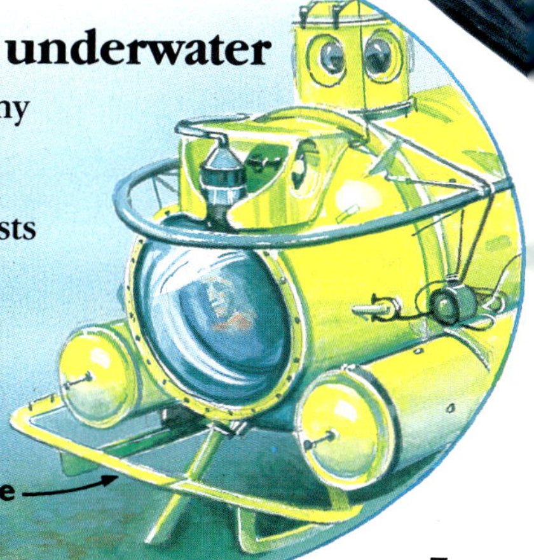

Submersible

7

Sea shores and coral reefs

Not all saltwater plants and animals live in the deep oceans. Many live on shores beside the sea, or in shallow water habitats, such as coral reefs. Plants and animals living on shores have to survive in a habitat that changes with the tides. They are under water when the tide is in. When it is out, they are in the open air.

Sandy shores

There are few hiding places on sandy shores. Small animals have to protect themselves so they do not get eaten.

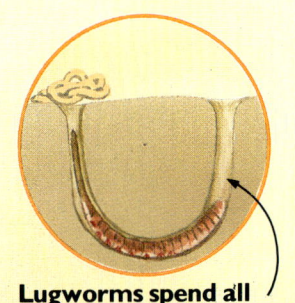

Shrimps have a hard covering and can burrow into the sand.

Turtles live in warm seas. They only come on to the shore to lay their eggs on sandy beaches. Many kinds of turtles are in danger of dying out.

Lugworms spend all their lives buried in the sand, in burrows.

Razorshells have a soft body and two long shells, joined along one side. Two muscles hold these shells closed if the razorshell is in danger.

BEACH ALARM
Many beaches are no longer safe for people or wildlife. They have been spoiled by pollution washed up from the sea, and by people dumping litter on them (see page 12).

Rocky shores

Animals living on rocky shores have plenty of hiding places. Many live in rock pools (pools left behind when the tide goes out).

Shore crabs have a hard shell, called a carapace. They shelter under rocks.

Limpets cling to rocks with a suction foot under their shells. This stops them from being swept away by the tide.

Seaweeds grow in shallow water. They cling to rocks, so they do not get washed away.

Sea anemones use their tentacles to catch shrimps and small fish.

Rock pool

Rock gobies hide in gaps between rocks.

Sea birds

Many birds feed on shores. They make their nests on cliffs, or on the beach.

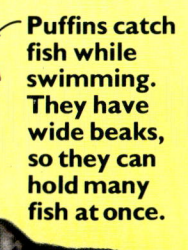

Puffins catch fish while swimming. They have wide beaks, so they can hold many fish at once.

Oystercatchers use their beaks to dig for shellfish, such as cockles.

Seagulls will eat almost anything. They even search for food on rubbish dumps.

Arctic terns dive into the water to catch fish. They can fly further than any other birds.

Coral reefs

Coral reefs are found in clear, shallow, warm seas. All kinds of colourful and unusual creatures live there. The reefs are made up of the shells of small animals, called coral polyps. As old polyps die, new ones grow on top of their empty shells.

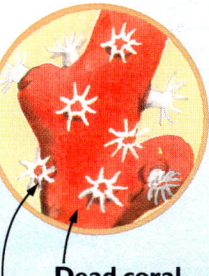

- Dead coral
- Living polyps
- Angel fish
- Humbugs
- Sea horses
- Clown fish
- Sea anemone
- Bridal burrfish
- Starfish
- Coral trout

Corals grow in many different shapes and colours. The oldest reefs began to form thousands of years ago. On pages 17 and 19, you can find out why reefs are now in danger.

Australia

The Great Barrier Reef is so large, it can even be seen from space.

The Great Barrier Reef

The Great Barrier Reef in Australia is over 2,000km (1,240 miles) long. It is the largest coral reef in the world. Over 2,000 different kinds of fish live there.

Pollution

On the next four pages, you can find out how water becomes polluted, and how this harms living things. You can also find out what has been done and what can be done to stop pollution and protect wildlife.

Factory waste

For many years, factories have been dumping huge amounts of waste into rivers and seas. This seemed to be a cheap and easy way of getting rid of it. People thought the waste would disappear. In fact, much of it stays in the water for a long time, and is a danger to humans and wildlife.

Waste pouring into rivers often contains harmful chemicals.

Some dangerous waste is dumped at the bottom of the sea.

Some waste is burned out at sea, in large ships. The ash is then dumped in the water.

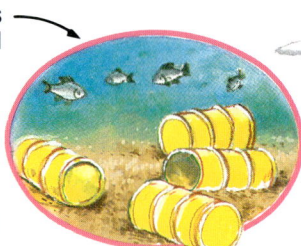

Belugas in trouble

Beluga whales live in the St Lawrence river, in Canada. This is one of the most polluted rivers in the world. Factories on its banks dump waste into the water. Many belugas have been poisoned.

Beluga whales are also called white whales.

In 1900, there were 5,000 belugas living in this river. Now there are less than 500.

Poisonous PCBs

PCBs are poisonous chemicals. When they are dumped in water, they are taken in by tiny plants and animals. When these are eaten by larger animals, the PCBs are taken in too. Animals, such as whales, at the top of the food chain, may eat many smaller poisoned ones. They then contain dangerous amounts of PCBs.

Factories use PCBs to cool machinery. PCBs have been banned in many countries but are still used in some places.

Dying seals

In 1988, over 18,000 common seals in the North Sea died of a disease. Most had PCBs in their bodies. Scientists have found that animals with PCBs in their bodies catch diseases easily.

People saved some seals by giving them injections against the disease.

In Germany, 30,000 people formed a human chain 40km (25 miles) long, across the island of Sylt, to protest against this pollution.

Pollution of groundwater

We cannot see groundwater, so it is hard to know when it has been polluted. Groundwater that is being polluted today may be used as drinking water in many years' time. Here are some of the ways this pollution can happen.

Waste from homes and factories is buried in large pits, called landfills.

Farmers spray their crops with chemicals, called pesticides, to kill insect pests.

Chemicals, and liquid from rotting waste can leak out and seep into groundwater.

Chemical fertilizers are put on fields to help crops grow.

All these chemicals may seep through soil into groundwater, and pollute it.

LOVE CANAL

From 1942 to 1953, 22,000 tonnes (24,000 tons) of chemicals were dumped at a place called Love Canal in the USA. In 1977, people living in houses that had been built on this land began to get strange illnesses. This was because chemicals had leaked into groundwater that was used as drinking water. 950 families had to move away from their homes.

Pollution facts

★ 20 billion tonnes (22 billion tons) of pollution are dumped into the oceans every year.

★ Sweden has 85,000 lakes. Over 21,000 of these, and about 100,000km (62,000 miles) of its streams and rivers have been polluted by acid rain (see right).

★ There are 400,000 landfills containing dangerous waste in the USA. 10,000 of these need to be made safer immediately.

Acid rain

When fuels, such as oil or coal, are burned in cars or factories, the waste gases mix with the water in air to make acid rain. North America and parts of Europe suffer most from acid rain.

Perch

When acid rain falls on lakes and rivers, it pollutes the water. Then many fish, such as perch and salmon, die.

Animals, such as otters, depend on fish for food. If there are no fish in a lake or river, the otters living there will starve.

More pollution

Not all pollution comes from factories or farms. Here are some other ways water becomes polluted.

Dirty beaches

Large amounts of human waste, or sewage, from toilets and drains, are dumped in the sea, often close to the shore. Sewage can be treated to make it safe, but many countries do not do this. Untreated sewage can cause all kinds of diseases.

Sewage washes up on to beaches, making them unsafe for swimming.

Making a living

Many people depend on the sea for food. In south-east Asia, one quarter of the people who live near the sea make a living from fishing. Their waters are some of the most polluted by sewage.

Shellfish take in a lot of pollution. In many places, they are no longer safe to eat.

Mussels
Lobsters
Crabs

Dumping rubbish

People dump all kinds of everyday rubbish on beaches and wetlands, or in rivers and ponds. Much of this can be dangerous.

Broken glass and the sharp edges of tin cans can cut people and animals.

Animals, such as turtles, can mistake plastic for food. It stays in their stomachs, making them feel full. They then stop eating, and can starve.

Oil pollution

When oil spills into the sea, it forms a large pool, called a slick, on the surface of the water. The slick can drift to shore, polluting beaches and killing wildlife. In 1991, during the Gulf War, up to two million barrels of oil leaked into the Persian Gulf, from oil wells in Kuwait.

Thousands of sea birds died because oil clogged their feathers, and they could no longer keep warm.

People saved some birds by washing the oil from their feathers.

Dugongs are rare animals that feed on seagrass. They could not eat seagrass covered in oil.

Whales may swallow plastic bags or balloons, thinking they are jellyfish.

Plastic rings that hold cans together can strangle birds, fish and other animals.

Time to stop polluting

Here are some of the ways people have tried to stop pollution. There are many things you can do to help (see pages 22-23). Everybody must work together to keep water clean and safe for people, plants and animals.

Saving Lake Baikal

◀ Lake Baikal is the oldest and deepest lake in the world. It is now being polluted by factories and farms around its shores. Local people are trying to protect the lake and its wildlife from pollution.

Many of Lake Baikal's animals are not found anywhere else.

This poster at a local bus station tells people about the problem. The message says "Save Lake Baikal".

Thirty per cent club

In 1985, 21 countries signed an agreement to try to stop acid rain. They plan to cut down the amount of poisonous gases from factories and power stations by almost one-third (thirty per cent) by 1993.

Rhine Action Plan

In 1980, four countries made the Rhine Action Plan, to try to clean up the River Rhine (see page 3). Factories must change the way they work, so that they make less waste.

Clean-up time

Earlier this century, the River Thames in London, England, was so polluted that no fish could live in it. In 1953, people began treating sewage before putting it into the river. Now 112 kinds of fish live there.

Radioactive waste

Radioactive waste, from nuclear power stations, can be very dangerous. It can change the way living things grow, and may cause cancer. Some radioactive waste stays harmful for thousands of years.

No more dumping

Some radioactive waste used to be sealed in barrels and dumped in the oceans. Then people realised that, one day, the barrels might break up, and the waste would escape. In 1983, all the world's countries agreed to ban the dumping of radioactive waste at sea.

Members of Greenpeace (see page 20) sailed near the dumping ships, to try to stop them from dropping the barrels. This helped many people to find out about the dangers.

Dangers from fishing

People have been fishing since the earliest times. Many still depend on fish for food, and to make a living. Today, fishermen can catch huge amounts of fish. On these pages, you can find out why this is not always a good thing.

Overfishing

If fishermen catch too many of one type of fish, that type can be in danger of dying out. This is called overfishing. When it happens, fishermen suffer as well, because they can no longer make a living.

Modern fishing boats

Modern fishing boats can catch up to 200 tonnes (220 tons) of fish at one time. Their large nets have small holes, so the fish cannot escape.

Trawl net

In 1976, there were so few herrings left in the North Sea that herring fishing was banned for 7 years to allow numbers to increase.

In Lake Victoria, in Africa, some tilapias are in danger from overfishing.

Overfishing does not happen when people agree to limit the number of fish they catch.

Catching krill

In the Southern Ocean, there are huge numbers of small animals called krill. They are an important part of the food chain there. Over the last ten years, some countries have started catching large amounts of krill. We must be careful not to overfish krill, as many other animals depend on them for food.

Some penguins catch krill while swimming in the Southern Ocean.

Crabeater seals living in Antarctica eat krill.

Krill are small shrimps.

Krill are the main food for baleen whales, such as minke whales.

In 1982, 35 countries made an agreement to try to protect krill from overfishing.

Dolphins and tuna

In the Eastern Pacific, dolphins and yellowfin tuna swim together. Dolphins swim near the surface and tuna swim a little way below.

When fishermen see dolphins, they know tuna may also be there. They put out nets to catch the tuna but many dolphins are caught too.

If nets had bigger holes, young fish could escape. They could then grow and breed, stopping numbers from getting too low.

The top of the net is on the surface of the water.

Purse-seine net

Dolphins and tuna swim into the net through the back.

When this rope is pulled from above, the two sides come together and the net closes.

Dolphins drown if they cannot reach the surface to breathe.

Some fishermen lower the net before pulling it in, so dolphins can swim out over the top.

Yellowfin tuna are a type of large fish.

Caught by mistake

Huge fishing nets, called drift-nets, which can be up to 56km (35 miles) long, are used in deep oceans. They are made of thin nylon, which is almost invisible in the water. All kinds of animals get trapped in them. Since 1991, drift-nets have been banned in the South Pacific.

Kemp's ridley turtles have almost died out, because so many have drowned in shrimp nets in the Gulf of Mexico.

Sea birds, such as albatrosses, dive into the water for fish, and get their feet or wings caught in nets.

Lost or torn nets of all types float through the oceans and carry on trapping animals, such as seals and small whales.

In the past 30 years, over five million dolphins have been killed in tuna nets – about one every three minutes. Many people think there should be a law protecting dolphins from being killed in this way. On page 23, you can find out how you can help to save them.

Hunting and collecting

People have always hunted water animals for their shells, skins, fur or meat. When too many of one type, or species, of animal are killed, that species can die out, or become extinct. Many species have already been hunted to extinction. Hundreds more are now in danger.

Beavers

100 years ago, North American beavers almost became extinct. They had been hunted so that their fur could be used to make hats. Laws were made to protect beavers, which saved them from extinction, but over half a million are still killed each year.

Baby beavers cannot survive if their mother is killed.

Whale hunting

Hundreds of years ago, people began hunting whales for their meat, and to make oil from their fat. First, slow swimmers, such as right whales, were hunted. Then, with faster boats, other whales could be caught too. Today, many species are in danger. On page 21, you can find out what people are doing to save whales.

Before hunting started, there were 100,000 right whales. Today, there are only about 3,000.

Turtles in trouble

Turtles are hunted for their meat and shells. Their eggs are dug up to be sold for food. All sea turtles, and some freshwater turtles, are now in danger of extinction.

Turtle shells are used to make jewellery and combs. Plastic copies look the same, but do not harm turtles.

Hawksbill, ridley and green turtles are all killed for their shells.

Hawksbill turtle

In Malaysia, people have set up a project to help leatherback turtles. Some of their eggs are dug up from the beach and taken to a safe place, called a sanctuary. When the baby turtles hatch, they are taken back to the same beach, and set free. ▶

Baby seals

In Canada, thousands of baby harp seals used to be killed every year, so that their fur could be made into coats. Many people thought this was cruel, and began to protest against it. There is now a law against killing these baby seals, but many older harp seals are still being killed.

Adult harp seal

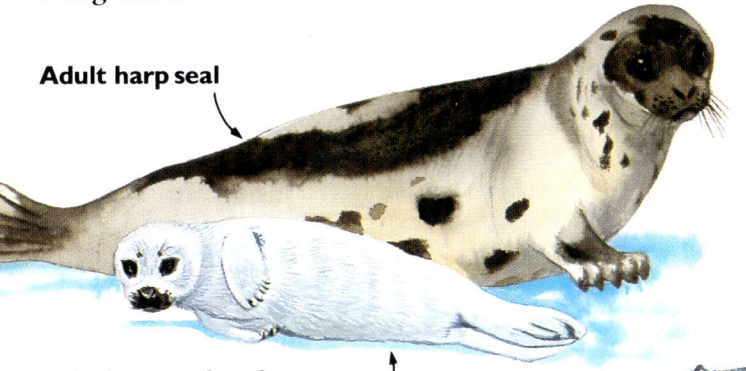

Baby harp seals only keep their beautiful, white coats for the first 15 days of their lives.

Crocodiles

In 1950, there were large numbers of crocodiles in some parts of the world. Then people started buying shoes, bags and belts made from their skins. Most species are now very rare because of this.

Gharials are river crocodiles which live in northern India. By 1974, there were fewer than 200 left. People are now trying to save gharials by hatching their eggs in sanctuaries.

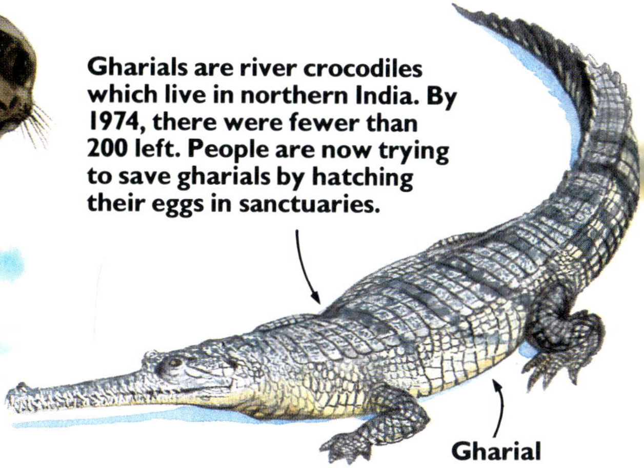

Gharial

Dangers from collecting

Some people collect unusual fish and keep them in tanks. Corals and shells are also collected, and made into jewellery or ornaments. These are sold to tourists, or to other countries. Many species are rare because of this.

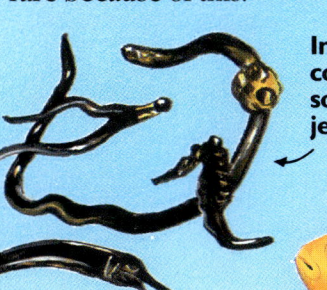

In the Caribbean Sea, black coral is almost extinct, because so much has been made into jewellery.

Some sea animals are collected so that their beautiful shells can be made into lamps or ornaments.

Off the coast of Malaysia, clown fish are in danger because so many have been collected.

Oysters and freshwater mussels are collected for the pearls inside their shells. Pearls are used to make jewellery, such as necklaces.

Changing habitats

The main reason that so many species are becoming extinct is that their habitats are being destroyed or disturbed by people.

Each species of plant or animal is suited to its living place. If this habitat changes, the species may not survive.

Habitat destruction

People destroy water habitats so they can make use of the land. Here are some of the ways this happens.

Rivers, ponds and wetlands are drained, and filled in with stones and soil to make the ground level.

Houses, shops and factories can be built on this new land.

Before | After

Farmers cut down trees, and other plants, from riverbanks, so that they have more room for fields.

Here are some of the plants and animals which are in danger because their habitats have been destroyed.

Storks lose their feeding places when wetlands are destroyed.

Lotuses in Egypt and southern marsh orchids in Britain are in danger because their marsh homes have been drained.

Lotus

Marsh orchid

Frogs and toads have nowhere to lay their eggs when their breeding ponds are filled in.

Toads on roads

Toads return to the same pond or lake each year, to lay their eggs. When busy roads are built along their routes, many toads are run over.

On some roads, there are signs warning drivers to look out for toads crossing.

Protected areas

Protected areas are places that have been set aside where plants and animals can live safely. People can go to most of them, but activities, such as fishing and building, are controlled, so as not to disturb wildlife. Protected sea areas are called marine reserves.

Threats from tourists

With modern transport, people can travel all over the world. Places that used to be quiet wildlife habitats are now popular holiday areas. Animals often suffer when this happens.

Baby turtles
Moonlight on the water helps baby turtles know which way to go to get to the sea. Bright lights from roads and buildings near the beach confuse them so that they set off in the wrong direction.

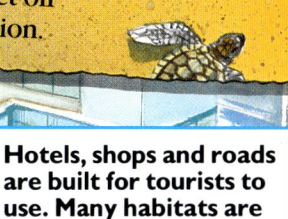

Monk seals
When tourists started going to beaches around the Mediterranean Sea, the monk seals living there were scared away. Today, there are only about 500 Mediterranean monk seals left.

Hotels, shops and roads are built for tourists to use. Many habitats are destroyed to make room for these.

Coral reefs
Coral reefs are easily harmed. Tourists can damage a reef with their feet, while swimming nearby. In south-east Asia, coral is dug up and used to make buildings, such as airports.

Wild animals are very nervous. They will not come near a beach if there are people sitting or playing on it.

Thousands of sea birds, such as frigatebirds, lay their eggs on Aldabra Atoll, a marine reserve in the Seychelles, in the Indian Ocean.

All kinds of unusual wildlife, such as greater flamingoes, live in the Camargue, a protected wetland area in southern France.

Motor boats make a lot of noise and their propellers can harm, or even kill, animals such as dolphins and seals.

Many more of these safe areas in or near water are needed, if we are going to protect habitats successfully.

Working towards a safer world

Many people are now trying to protect water habitats and the wildlife living there, so that plants and animals can live in a safer world. Below, you can find out about how they are doing this, and about some of the species that have been protected.

Conservation groups

There are many groups working to protect water. They tell people about the dangers and set up projects to save species. Some try to get laws passed to stop hunting, pollution and so on.

Groups, such as Greenpeace and Friends of the Earth, often carry out unusual actions, to draw people's attention to problems, and to raise money.

Friends of the Earth has a globe as its symbol.

These members of Greenpeace hung on ropes from a bridge over the River Rhine, to protest against pollution.

Seal success

In 1900, there were fewer than 100 northern elephant seals left, because of hunting. In 1972, a law was passed in the USA, making it illegal to kill these seals. Today, thousands breed every year at the Año Nuevo State Reserve, a wildlife park in California, USA.

Elephant seals are the largest seal species.

Peace for Antarctica

In 1959, 16 countries signed the Antarctic Treaty, to try to protect Antarctica from pollution and disturbance. One of the things they had to decide was whether to allow mining. In 1991, they agreed that no mining was to be allowed in Antarctica for at least 50 years.

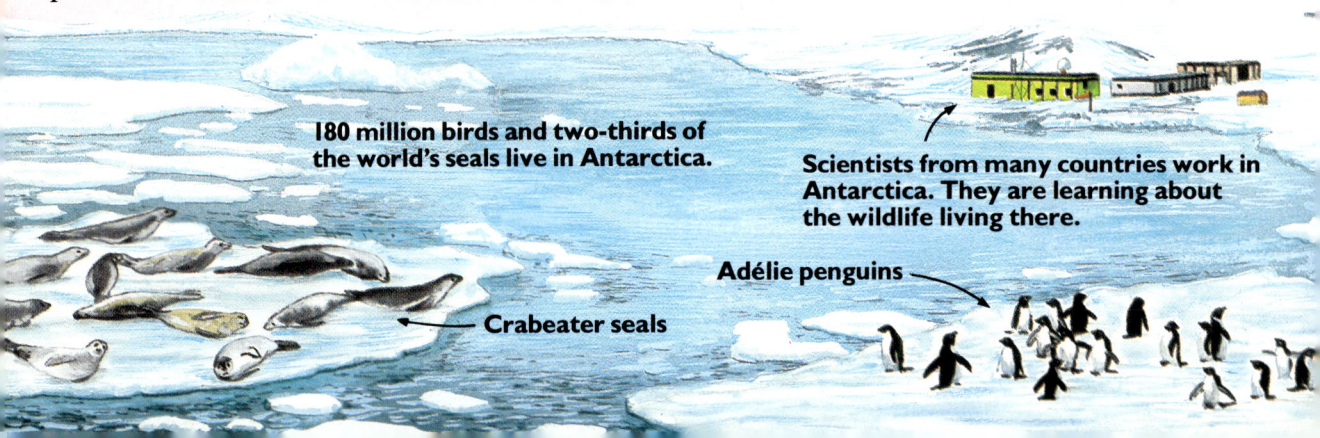

180 million birds and two-thirds of the world's seals live in Antarctica.

Scientists from many countries work in Antarctica. They are learning about the wildlife living there.

Crabeater seals

Adélie penguins

Protected pelicans

Brown pelicans nest on Pelican Island, in Florida, USA. People are not allowed to visit the island, in case they disturb the birds.

In the 1960s, brown pelicans in the USA were in danger because they were eating fish that had been poisoned by pesticides. In 1972, these pesticides were banned. Since then, the number of pelicans has greatly increased.

Saving whales

By the 1970s, many species of whales were in great danger because of hunting. In 1986, 36 countries agreed to ban the hunting of larger whales. Every year, they meet to decide whether to continue this ban. They also have to decide whether smaller whales need protection too.

People hope the ban will help to save whales, such as humpbacks, from becoming extinct.

Laws and agreements

★ In Florida, USA, local people have made laws to keep beach lighting low at turtle-nesting times (see page 19).

★ In the Seychelles, anyone who kills or harms a sea mammal can be sent to prison for up to five years.

★ Since 1988, 31 countries have agreed to ban their ships from dumping plastic rubbish into the sea.

★ In 1976, 18 countries signed the Mediterranean Action Plan, to try to clean up the Mediterranean Sea, one of the most polluted in the world.

Balicasag Island

In 1985, a marine reserve was set up on Balicasag Island, in the Philippines. Local people took part in starting up the reserve and now help to run it.

They put up information signs and tell tourists about the area. They are also learning ways of making a living which do not harm wildlife.

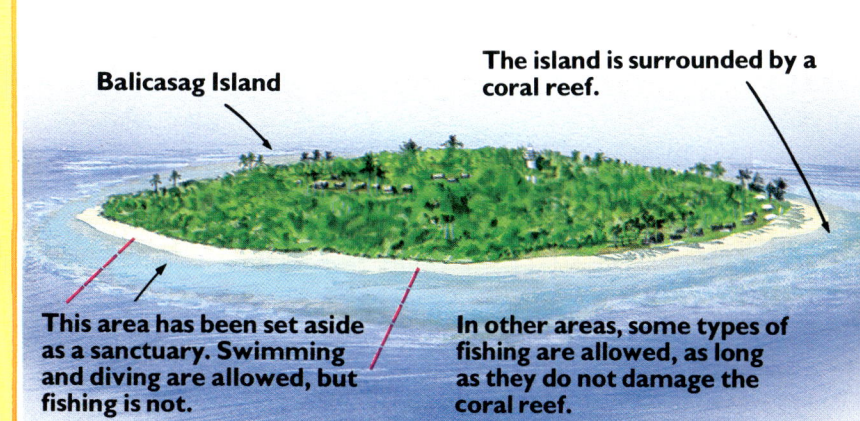

Balicasag Island

The island is surrounded by a coral reef.

This area has been set aside as a sanctuary. Swimming and diving are allowed, but fishing is not.

In other areas, some types of fishing are allowed, as long as they do not damage the coral reef.

What you can do

There are many things we can all do to protect the world's water. Here are some ideas. Everyone can do something to help.

Make less waste

All the rubbish from homes, schools and offices has to be put somewhere. A lot is buried underground and this can pollute groundwater (see page 11). You can help to reduce this pollution by making less waste.

Save paper by writing on both sides of every sheet.

Used batteries leak harmful chemicals. Try using rechargeable ones instead. They contain chemicals too, but can be re-used many times.

Plastic containers, such as ice-cream tubs, can be re-used for storing things.

Many of the things we buy are packaged in layers of paper and plastic. Try to buy things which have less packaging.

Fast-food restaurants often use a lot of packaging, which is thrown away almost immediately.

Before you throw something away, make sure that you really cannot use it any more.

Recycling

Glass, metal and most kinds of paper can be recycled (turned back into new glass, metal or paper). You could collect used bottles, cans and paper at home and at school. Your local authority or conservation group will have information about recycling in your area.

Look out for this symbol on things such as paper and cans. It means that they can be recycled.

In many towns, there are special bins where you can put glass bottles, cans or newspapers to be recycled.

Saving water

The less water you use, the less dirty water goes down the drain. This means there is less sewage to be poured into rivers and seas. Here are some ways to save water.

- Try not to leave the water running while you brush your teeth. Only turn it on to rinse your brush.
- If you can, have showers instead of baths. They use about half as much water.
- Ask an adult to mend dripping taps. One leaking tap could fill 52 baths in a year.

Balloons and bags

If balloons and plastic bags end up in the sea, they can harm water animals (see page 12). You can help in the following ways.

Try not to let go of balloons when you are outdoors. The wind may carry them to the sea.

Re-use plastic bags as much as possible or, even better, go shopping with a canvas bag or basket instead.

Dolphin-friendly tuna

You can now buy cans of tuna fish which are labelled to say that dolphins were not harmed when the tuna was caught.

Look for labels like this.

If your local shops do not sell dolphin-friendly tuna, ask them why. Tell them you will only buy this kind of tuna.

Safer waste

You can also help to protect water and the wildlife living there by making some kinds of waste safer before throwing them away, or washing them down the drain.

Cut up the plastic rings that hold cans together before you put them in the bin. Then they cannot harm animals (see page 12).

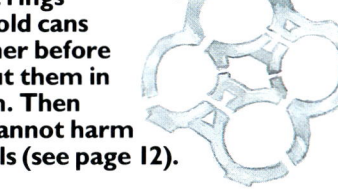

Some cleaning products have harmful chemicals in them. Waste water containing these chemicals can end up in the sea. Try to get your family to buy safer products.

Litter

Litter dropped on a beach, near a river or from a boat can harm water animals. Always put litter in a bin, or take it home instead. Even if you are not near water, litter can be carried a long way by the wind. Every bit makes a difference.

Taking action

Local conservation groups often get together to clean up beaches, or areas near rivers, ponds and lakes. There are some groups especially for children. Your local library should have information about groups in your area.

Always make sure there is an adult with you when you go near water.

23

Index

acid rain, 11, 13
Antarctica, 6, 14, 20

beavers, 5, 16
birds,
    albatrosses, 15
    Arctic terns, 9
    flamingoes, 19
    frigatebirds, 19
    kingfishers, 4
    oystercatchers, 9
    pelicans, brown, 21
    penguins, 6, 14, 20
    puffins, 9
    seagulls, 9
    storks, 5, 18

chemicals, 10, 11, 22, 23
collecting, 16-17
conservation groups, 13, 20, 22, 23
coral, 3, 8-9, 17, 19, 21
crabs, 8, 12
crocodiles, 4, 17

dolphins, 7, 15, 19, 23
dragonflies, 4
dugongs, 12

factories, 3, 10, 11, 13, 18
farming, 11, 13, 18
fish,
    angler fish, 7
    bitterling, 4
    carp, 4
    clown fish, 9, 17
    herrings, 7, 14
    perch, 4, 11
    rock gobies, 8

salmon, 4, 11
sharks, 7
tilapias, 14
tuna, 6, 15, 23
fishing, 6, 12, 14-15, 18, 21
food chains, 5, 7, 10, 14
frogs, 4, 5, 18

Great Barrier Reef, 9
groundwater, 2, 11, 22
Gulf War, 12

habitats, 3, 4, 5, 6, 8
    destruction of, 18-19
hippopotamuses, 4
hunting, 16-17, 20, 21

krill, 14

landfills, 11
limpets, 8
litter, 8, 23
lotuses, 18
lugworms, 8

marine reserves, 18-19, 21
mussels, 12, 17

octopuses, 6
orchids, southern marsh, 18
otters, 4, 11
oysters, 17

PCBs, 10
pesticides, 11, 21
plankton, 7
plastic, 12, 16, 21, 22, 23
polar bears, 6
pollution, 3, 10-13, 20, 22

protected areas, 18-19

razorshells, 8
recycling, 22
rock pools, 8
rubbish, 9, 12, 21, 22

sanctuaries, 16, 17, 21
sea anemones, 8, 9
seals, 6, 15
    common, 10
    crabeater, 14, 20
    elephant, 20
    harp, 17
    Mediterranean monk, 19
seaweeds, 8
sewage, 12, 13, 22
shellfish, 6, 9, 12
shells, 17
shrimps, 5, 8, 14
submersible, 7

toads, 5, 18
tourists, 17, 19, 21
turtles, 8, 12, 16, 19
    green, 16
    hawksbill, 16
    leatherback, 16
    ridley, 15, 16

waste, 3, 10-13, 22-23
water cycle, 2
wetlands, 4-5, 18, 19
whales, 7, 12, 16, 21
    beluga, 10
    humpback, 7, 21
    minke, 14
    right, 16

First published in 1991 by Usborne Publishing Ltd, 83-85 Saffron Hill, London, EC1N 8RT, England. Copyright © 1991 Usborne Publishing Ltd. All rights reserved. No part of this publication may be reproduced, stored in a retrieval system, or transmitted by any means, electronic, mechanical, photocopying, recording or otherwise, without the prior permission of the publisher. The name Usborne and the device are the Trade Marks of Usborne Publishing Ltd. UE